I'm NOT Moving!

Written by Wiley Blevins
Illustrated by Mattia Cerato

Please visit our website at www.redchairpress.com.
Find a free catalog of all our high-quality products for young readers.

I'm Not Moving!
Publisher's Cataloging-In-Publication Data
(Prepared by The Donohue Group, Inc.)

Blevins, Wiley.

I'm not moving! / written by Wiley Blevins ; illustrated by Mattia Cerato.
p. : col. ill. ; cm. -- (Family snaps)
Summary: When Keesha's dad gets a new job, her family has to move to the city. Keesha finds that change is hard when it means leaving behind the home she loves and moving to a new house, a new school, and meeting new friends.
Interest age level: 005-008.
Issued also as an ebook.
ISBN: 978-1-939656-08-7 (lib. binding/hardcover)
ISBN: 978-1-939656-64-3 (pbk.)
ISBN: 978-1-939656-09-4 (eBk)
1. Moving, Household--Juvenile fiction. 2. Change--Juvenile fiction. 3. Adjustment (Psychology) in children--Juvenile fiction. 4. Moving, Household--Fiction. 5. Change--Fiction. 6. Adjustment (Psychology)--Fiction. I. Cerato, Mattia. II. Title.
PZ7.B618652 Im 2014

[E] 2013956079

First published by:
Red Chair Press LLC PO Box 333 South Egremont, MA 01258-0333

Printed in the United States of America

1 2 3 4 5 18 17 16 15 14

Dad got off the phone
and jumped up and down.
"I got it!" he yelled.
"Got what?" I asked.
"The measles?"

"I got the job," said Dad.

Mom gave him a big hug.

"We're moving to the city!" she said.

I crossed my arms.

"We're moving where?"

"I'm not moving," I said.

"My friends and school are here. Not in the city."

Mom handed me a box.

"I'm not **moving**," I said.

"My horse is here.

In the city they only have rats.

Big, mean subway rats."

Dad handed me a bag.

"I'm not **moving**," I said.

"My dance class is here.

In the city they don't wear pink tutus.

Like mine."

"Get in the car,"

Mom and Dad said.

We drove past the farm I love.

We drove past the woods I love.

And we drove past the lake I love.

until...

...the city. Ugh!

Mom handed me a small box.

"What's this?" I asked.

"It's all your special things," she said.

"Let's put them in your new room," said Dad.

"You can paint it any color," said Dad.

I chose pink.

Then I painted trees and a lake on the wall.

I even painted a horse.

"It's still not **home**," I said.

"Let's go for a walk," said Dad.
He took me to a big park.
Right in the middle of the city.
It had a small zoo in it.

"No horses?" I asked.

"No," said Dad. "But it does have seals."

"You can't ride a seal," I said.

"I have a surprise for you," said Mom.
"Put on your dance clothes."

Mom took me to a big building.

"See all the dance classes!" she said.

"Yes," I said. "But no one is dressed like me."

"Tomorrow you start a new school," said Dad.

"You need to get some sleep," said Mom.

"I'm not **going**," I said.

"Wake up!" yelled Mom.

"We don't want to be late," said Dad.

"I'm not **going**," I said.

My new teacher smiled at me.

I crossed my arms.

"Sit at any computer," she said.

"I get my own computer?" I asked.

"WOW!"

"Hi," said a girl. "I'm Emma."

She wore a shirt with horses on it.

"Hi," said another girl. "I'm Grace."
She wore black pants. And a **pink tutu.**

"Welcome to our class," they said.

"Do you like your new home?" they asked.
We danced around the desks.
"I think I do now!"